Winky Blue Forever

by Pamela Jane
illustrated by Debbie Tilley

To the children at Marcus Hook Elementary School, and with special thanks to David and Penny at Black Tie Balloons and Rob Burke from Mercurial Video Productions—P.J.

For my cousin, Mary Beth—D.T.

Text copyright © 1999 by Pamela Jane
Illustrations copyright © 1999 by Debbie Tilley

For information contact:
MONDO Publishing
One Plaza Road
Greenvale, New York 11548
MONDO is a registered trademark of Mondo Publishing
Visit our web site at http://www.mondopub.com

Printed in the United States of America
99 00 01 02 03 04 05 06   9 8 7 6 5 4 3 2 1

Design by Janet Pedersen
Production by The Kids at Our House

Library of Congress Cataloging-in-Publication Data
Jane, Pamela.
    Winky Blue forever / by Pamela Jane ; illustrated by Debbie Tilley.
        p.   cm.
    Summary: Rosie plans to make her parakeet Winky Blue famous forever through a series of television commercials, but her hopes are crushed when he is lost on the way into New York City.
    ISBN 1-57255-624-2 (pbk. : alk. paper)
    [1. Parakeets—Fiction. 2. Pets—Fiction. 3. Lost and found possessions—Fiction. 4. New York (N.Y.)—Fiction.] I. Tilley, Debbie, ill. II. Title.
PZ7.J213Wi   1999
[Fic]—dc21   98-45379
                                                                                CIP
                                                                                AC

Contents

A Wish and a Whoosh!

Rosie lay in her backyard watching the gold-tinged leaves of the maple tree wave gently against the blue sky.

"What I really, *really* wish," Rosie murmured dreamily, "is that Winky Blue would become famous."

"Cheep. Right on!" answered Winky from his cage on Rosie's screened-in porch.

"Winky *is* famous," said Michael. Michael was sitting on the grass with Rosie and Eliza. Eliza's dog, Raffles, was stretched out beside them, snoring.

"That's right," said Eliza. "Winky was on TV when he saved Cinnamon from falling off the top of the Empire State Building."

Cinnamon, Michael's pet gerbil, poked his head out of Michael's shirt sleeve and twitched his whiskers.

"Winky was a hero and a star," said Michael, scratching Cinnamon behind his ears. "That's what you always wanted, Rosie."

It was true. Ever since Rosie and her Aunt Maria had moved from their tiny apartment to the house on Lincoln Avenue, Rosie had dreamed of owning a famous pet, like Lassie. And last year, when she saw the blue parakeet at Wags 'n' Whiskers Pet Shop, Rosie knew he was the one for her.

"But Winky was only a star for one day and then everyone forgot about him," said Rosie. "I want Winky to be famous forever."

"My dad says nothing is forever," said Eliza.

"Yucky!" yelled Winky from the porch.

Michael and Eliza laughed. *Yucky* was

Winky's favorite new word.

Rosie sighed and gazed up at the cloudless September sky. "If only something wonderful would happen to make Winky famous forever," she said.

"Things don't just happen out of the blue," said Michael.

Just then Rosie heard a loud noise overhead. Raffles woke up and started barking.

"Look, something's coming out of the sky!" cried Eliza.

Rosie jumped to her feet. If Martians were about to land in her backyard, she wanted to be ready. But it wasn't a spaceship that came sailing over the housetops. It was a giant, rainbow-colored balloon.

"It's a hot-air balloon!" cried Michael. "See the flame."

Whoosh! A huge flame shot up into the balloon with a loud noise. And hanging on the side of the balloon basket was a sign.

"Ruff ruff," barked Raffles.

The screen door slammed as Aunt Maria ran outside.

"What's that noise?" she asked.

"It's a hot-air balloon!" shouted Rosie.

People from all over the neighborhood came running to see the balloon up close. The balloon pilot waved as he glided over Eliza's house next door.

"Look out down there!" the pilot yelled. "I'm going to land."

Everyone hurried to Rosie's driveway to make room for the giant balloon—everyone, except Rosie. She raced back to the porch and grabbed Winky's cage.

Something magical and exciting was about to happen, right in her own backyard. Rosie was going to make sure Winky Blue was right in the middle of it.

Out of the Blue

Whoosh! The hot-air balloon sailed into Rosie's backyard, tickling the top of the maple tree. Dogs barked and children yelled as the gigantic balloon floated down, down, down until it came to rest gently on the grass.

Just as the balloon touched down, a truck screeched to a halt in front of Rosie's house. Three people jumped out wearing caps that said Bill's Balloon Team.

"Great!" shouted the balloon pilot. "My crew is here."

The crew helped steady the balloon as a young man climbed out of the basket.

"Well," said Aunt Maria. "This is a surprise."

"It's a surprise for me, too," said the man, smiling. "In a hot-air balloon, you never know exactly where you're going until you get there."

"It's just like in *The Wizard of Oz*," said Eliza, in awe.

The man laughed. "I'm not from Oz, and I'm certainly not a wizard," he said. "My name is Bill Burke."

"I can't believe you landed here, right in my backyard!" said Rosie.

"This is your backyard?" asked Bill.

Rosie nodded. "And this is my bird, Winky Blue," she said, proudly holding up Winky's cage.

Bill held out his finger to Winky. "Pleased to meet you, Winky Blue," he said.

"Right on!" chirped Winky as he stuck his claw through the bars of his cage and "shook hands" with Bill. Then Bill reached into his backpack and pulled out a big paper bag.

"Cider and donuts, anyone?" he asked. "I

always celebrate after a successful flight."

Aunt Maria brought out paper plates and cups, and everyone had a picnic in Rosie's backyard.

"Yucky. No way. Yummy!" chattered Winky, nibbling on a chocolate donut.

"That's a smart bird you have there," said Bill.

Rosie beamed. "You can say that again."

"Smart bird!" said Winky.

Bill looked thoughtfully at Winky.

"Wags 'n' Whiskers is looking for a pet to make a television ad," he said. "A smart bird like Winky might be just the pet for the job."

Michael whistled. "Wow, Winky on TV!"

Rosie said nothing. She was very quiet. Rosie always got quiet when she was *really* excited. And she was really excited now.

Rosie had wished for something wonderful to happen, and her wish had come true. A rainbow-colored balloon had sailed out of the sky with a burst of flame and the promise of fame for Winky Blue.

Action!

That night Rosie dreamed Winky was soaring over the rainbow in a brightly-colored balloon. It was an exciting dream, but what happened Monday after school was even better.

Rosie was giving Winky a ride on his bird-sized bike when Aunt Maria called down the hall.

"Rosie! Mr. Blackwell is on the phone. He wants to talk to you right away."

Mr. Blackwell was the owner of Wags 'n' Whiskers Pet Shop. Rosie hurried down the hall with Winky perched on her shoulder.

15

"Hello, Rosie. Bill Burke told me about how he met you and Winky Blue," said Mr. Blackwell when Rosie answered. "It looks like that bird of yours has turned out pretty special."

"Oh, no," said Rosie. "Winky didn't turn out special. He was special right from the start."

Mr. Blackwell laughed. "That's great, Rosie," he said. "And that's why I'd like Winky Blue to be the Wags 'n' Whiskers spokesperson—I mean spokesbird—*if* he can follow directions."

"Winky can follow directions," said Rosie eagerly. "He's very smart. He says 'yummy' when I give him the thumbs-up sign and 'yucky' when I give the thumbs-down sign."

"That's great," said Mr. Blackwell, "because I want Winky to make a television ad for our special Super Birdseed Treat."

"Right on!" Winky shouted.

"'Right on' is right," said Mr. Blackwell. "Now I'd like you to bring Winky to the store on Saturday. We want to do a test shoot to see how he performs under the bright lights."

"Winky will perform perfectly," said Rosie. "He's a star, Mr. Blackwell."

Rosie meant that. She knew Winky would be great. But just to make absolutely sure, Rosie and Michael put Winky under Aunt Maria's reading lamp to get him used to bright lights.

"No way! Yucky!" said Winky, blinking in the glare of the lights.

"It's like in the movies," said Michael. "When the cops want to get crooks to tell the truth, they shine light in their eyes."

"Winky always tells the truth," said Rosie, looking lovingly at her bird. "And now he is going to be a star forever."

On Friday night, Rosie gave Winky his weekly bath. When he was all fluffy and dry, she covered his cage for the night.

"Tonight, sleep," Rosie whispered to Winky. "Tomorrow, stardom!"

Early Saturday morning, a big crowd was waiting in front of Wags 'n' Whiskers. Rosie had told everyone at school about the TV ad.

The crew was busy moving microphones and lights. Mr. Blackwell was running around, shouting out orders.

"Rosie, put Winky on that table between the two bowls of birdseed," Mr. Blackwell said. "Everyone else, stay behind the rope."

"Good luck, Winky Blue!" called Aunt Maria as Rosie put Winky on the table in a pool of light.

Winky didn't seem to mind being in the spotlight. He cocked his head, eyeing the two heaping bowls of birdseed. One bowl was labeled BRAND X BIRDSEED. The other was labeled WAGS 'N' WHISKERS SUPER BIRDSEED TREAT.

"Quiet on the set!" shouted Mr. Blackwell. "We're about to begin filming. Rosie, keep your eyes on Winky. As soon as he nibbles the Brand X birdseed, make him say 'yucky.' "

"That's easy," said Rosie. "All I have to do is give him the thumbs-down sign."

"Good," said Mr. Blackwell. "But this is the tricky part. The second Winky goes for the Wags 'n' Whiskers Super Birdseed Treat, signal him to say 'yummy' loud and clear. Got it?"

Rosie nodded, her heart pounding. This was it. The big test. If Winky passed, he would be famous forever.

And if he didn't pass? Rosie didn't want to think about that.

"Ready?" shouted Mr. Blackwell. "Roll tape . . . action!"

Thumbs Down, Winky Blue

Everyone stopped talking. Even the parakeets and canaries stopped singing in their cages. The lights and cameras were all focused on Winky.

The video tape started to roll.

Right on cue, Winky began nibbling the Brand X birdseed. When he looked up, Rosie quickly gave the thumbs-down sign. But Winky paid no attention.

"Yummy. Right on!" Winky said loudly. Then he sampled the Wags 'n' Whiskers Super Birdseed Treat.

"Yucky!" he shouted.

"Cut!" bellowed Mr. Blackwell.

The cameras stopped rolling.

"That bird is all mixed up," Mr. Blackwell shouted. "He said my birdseed was yucky and the other brand was yummy!"

Rosie felt her face turning red. This was a test shoot, and Winky had flunked.

"Please, can we try again?" Rosie pleaded. "I'm sure Winky didn't mean it."

"Cheep," said Winky sadly.

"I'll give Winky one more chance," said Mr. Blackwell. "Ready everyone . . . roll it!"

"Please, Winky, do it right," Rosie whispered under her breath.

But the next time was even worse. Winky ignored Rosie's hand signals, knocked over the microphone, and spilled birdseed all over the table.

"Right on. Watch out!" chattered Winky, bobbing up and down.

"Winky Blue is not cooperating," Mr. Blackwell said, frowning. "We'd better get the shot gun."

A shocked silence fell over the crowd.

"The shot gun?" Rosie gasped. "You can't shoot my bird!"

Winky Shoots to Fame

Aunt Maria put her arm around Rosie.

"Rosie, no one is going to shoot Winky," she said.

"Of course not," said Mr. Blackwell. "I'm talking about the shot gun microphone. It's a special microphone that Winky won't be able to knock over."

The new microphone worked wonderfully, but it couldn't make Winky say the right words.

Mr. Blackwell looked serious. "Maybe we'd better find another pet food star," he said.

Zachary suggested his pet canary, Ambrose, and Jasmine volunteered her goldfish, Tuna.

"Wait," said Michael. "Maybe Winky just has his signals crossed. Try giving him the thumbs-up sign for *yucky* and thumbs-down sign for *yummy*."

Sure enough, when Rosie switched her signals, Winky performed perfectly. He yelled "yucky" loud and clear for the Brand X birdseed and "yummy" for the Wags 'n' Whiskers brand.

"Cut!" yelled Mr. Blackwell. "Excellent! We'll use this take for the ad."

"Winky is a winner!" cried Rosie. "He just had his signals mixed up."

"Mixed up. Fixed up!" chattered Winky.

Mr. Blackwell smiled broadly. "The ad will air next week on Channel 67," he said. "Winky will be on every television set in Oakdale."

"Sixty-seven, sixty-seven, sixty-seven," Rosie repeated over and over to herself. She was sure sixty-seven was her lucky number.

Rising Stars

The Wags 'n' Whiskers ad was a big hit. In hundreds of homes, people laughed when they heard Winky Blue say "yummy" and "yucky."

Winky was a television star, but Rosie was the star in school. Everyone at Oakdale Elementary wanted to meet Winky. Rosie, Michael, and Eliza passed out free tickets, and kids lined up outside Rosie's house, waiting their turns to see the famous parakeet in person.

Winky just sat on his perch with his feathers puffed up, enjoying the attention.

At school the words *yummy* and *yucky* rang through the halls and cafeteria. Mrs. Lowe, the cook, put her hands over her ears.

"If I hear anyone say 'yummy' or 'yucky' one more time, I'll scream!" she screamed.

But Mr. Blackwell was happy. His Super Birdseed Treat was selling so fast he couldn't keep it on the shelves.

"We have to make another ad quick," he told Rosie when she stopped by Wags 'n' Whiskers to buy Winky a new cuttlebone. "And this time we'll do it in a big New York advertising studio."

"Can Michael and Eliza come, too?" Rosie asked.

Mr. Blackwell smiled. "Sure, if their parents say it's all right. There will be plenty of room. We're going in a limousine."

A limousine! Rosie was awestruck. Winky wasn't just a star. He was a super, shining star.

Early Saturday morning a long black limousine pulled up in front of Rosie's house. Inside there was room for everyone—Rosie, Aunt Maria, Mr. Blackwell, Michael, Eliza, Raffles, and of course, Winky Blue.

The limousine glided down the quiet streets of

Oakdale. Soon they were whizzing along on the highway past cars and buses and noisy trucks.

Rosie opened Winky's travel cage and let him sit on her shoulder.

"New York City, here we come!" she sang.

Rosie remembered the last time she had taken Winky to New York. He had become a hero and a star, but just for a day.

This time will be different, thought Rosie as they sped along. *This time is forever.*

Rosie leaned back happily and looked around the limousine. There was a telephone, a snack bar with drinks and pretzels, and even a tiny TV set.

Michael was more interested in the panel of shiny buttons above their heads.

"Look at all these controls," he said. "It's just like a spaceship."

"I wonder what this one does," said Rosie, pressing a round silver button.

Instantly, the sun roof opened and a powerful blast of wind sucked Winky right out through the top of the limousine.

9-1-1

"Oh, no! WINKY!" cried Rosie. "We have to stop!"

"Slow down and pull over!" Mr. Blackwell shouted to the limousine driver.

"Now everyone stay calm, and stay in the car," said Aunt Maria as the limousine pulled over to the side of the highway.

Rosie stood on the back seat and stuck her head out the sun roof.

"Winky! Winky, come back!" she shouted. But her voice was drowned out by the roar of the traffic speeding by.

"Winky! Winky Blue!" Michael and Eliza yelled out the windows.

Mr. Blackwell picked up the mobile telephone and dialed 9-1-1. "Put out a bird alert immediately. The Wags 'n' Whiskers parakeet has escaped!"

Rosie was stunned. Winky had been lost before, but never like this. The highway was fast and dangerous. There was no place for a frightened bird to find safety.

"Winky, where are you? Winky, come back!" Rosie shouted until she was hoarse.

Mr. Blackwell got out of the limousine and walked up and down the side of the highway calling for Winky.

After a while, Mr. Blackwell returned to the car. "We can't make a birdseed ad without a bird. We'll have to turn around and go home."

"But we can't go home without Winky!" cried Rosie.

"Don't worry, Rosie," said Aunt Maria. "We'll make posters and put an ad in the newspaper with a reward for finding Winky."

Tears rolled down Rosie's face as the limousine pulled away. Going home felt like giving up. And giving up on Winky Blue was something Rosie would never, ever do.

Bigger and Bigger and Bigger

That night Rosie slept on the living room couch so she wouldn't see Winky's cage standing sad and empty in her bedroom.

"Don't give up hope, Rosie," Aunt Maria said when she gave Rosie her goodnight hug. "As long as this warm weather holds up, Winky has a good chance of surviving."

Rosie nodded, but she didn't say what was in her mind. *What if the warm weather doesn't hold up? What if there is a frost or a sudden cold snap?*

Rosie knew she had to act fast if she wanted to save Winky.

The next day after school, Rosie and Aunt Maria went to the mall. Rosie used her birthday money to buy a new sweatshirt. On the back of the sweatshirt the sales clerk printed a picture of Winky and an announcement.

LOST

BEAUTIFUL BLUE PARAKEET NEAR OAKDALE, NEW JERSEY. CALL ROSIE 555-0829

Rosie wore the sweatshirt everywhere. Aunt Maria helped her put up "missing" posters, too. Mr. Blackwell placed an ad in the *Daily Herald* offering a reward for finding Winky Blue.

But no one called.

"I wish I had wings," Rosie said to Michael on the way home from school a few days later. "Then I could fly high above the trees and look for Winky."

Michael stopped in the middle of the sidewalk and stared at Rosie.

"Rosie, we *can* fly," Michael said, "in Bill Burke's hot-air balloon."

"Michael," said Rosie. "You're a genius."

Rosie and Michael raced home to call Bill. Aunt Maria helped them look up his phone number.

"Sure," Bill said when Rosie reached him. "I'll take you up on Saturday morning if the wind and weather are right."

"Yes!" whispered Michael, who was listening on the extension.

"We'll take off from a schoolyard near the

highway where Winky disappeared," Bill said before he hung up.

It rained on Friday night, but the sun was peeking out from behind the clouds when Rosie and Aunt Maria arrived at the schoolyard with Michael and Eliza on Saturday morning. Bill's Balloon Team was already in action, blowing up the giant balloon. Raffles barked as the balloon grew bigger and bigger and bigger.

"All right, everyone get in," said Bill when the balloon was ready.

"Not me," said Aunt Maria. "I'll stay right here on planet Earth."

Rosie couldn't wait to get off planet Earth and high up into the blue sky.

Everyone climbed into the balloon basket, including Raffles.

Whoosh! The gas flame leaped up and the balloon rose slowly into the air. Rosie, Michael, and Eliza waved to Aunt Maria and the Balloon Team.

"Goodbye everyone! Goodbye Earth!" Michael and Eliza shouted.

"Hello Winky," whispered Rosie. She crossed her fingers for good luck.

Lost Forever?

Aunt Maria and the schoolyard grew smaller and smaller as the balloon sailed up, up, up above the green and gold trees. Far below dogs barked at the balloon. Raffles barked back.

"Over that way is New York City," said Bill, pointing to the dim outline of buildings in the far distance.

"And look," said Michael. "There's a rainbow!"

"It must have been raining in New York, too," said Bill.

Eliza started to sing. "Some-where, o-ver-the-rain-bow, blue-birds-fly . . ."

"I wish we could fly over the rainbow and find Winky," said Rosie.

The sun rose higher. Rosie checked to make sure her Winky Blue sweatshirt was still hanging over the side of the balloon basket.

Bill handed Rosie a pair of binoculars.

"I'm going to fly low over the trees," Bill said. "You look through the binoculars to see if you spot Winky."

"Winky! Winky Blue!" Rosie, Michael, and Eliza called and called. But there was no flash of blue, no happy "Chirp!" from Winky. The only sounds were the sputter of the pilot light in the balloon and the creaking of the wicker basket that carried them along.

Bill picked up his two-way radio and contacted the Balloon Team on the ground.

"Charlene, do you read me? The wind is picking up. I'm going to land near that farm across the road."

Charlene's voice came back over the radio. "Roger," she said. "Over and out."

Rosie couldn't believe it. The balloon ride was almost over and they hadn't found Winky.

Just then a gust of wind picked up Rosie's Winky Blue sweatshirt and whisked it away.

"Hey, my sweatshirt!" yelled Rosie.

"Look. It landed in the back of that pick-up truck," said Michael, peering over the side of the balloon basket.

"Stop! Stop!" Rosie yelled at the truck. But the truck rolled on down the highway.

"My sweatshirt is gone forever," said Rosie sadly.

Rosie lost more than her sweatshirt on the balloon ride that morning. She lost her hopes of finding Winky Blue over the rainbow.

Over the Rainbow

Winky had been missing for over a week, but more people than ever were watching the Wags 'n' Whiskers television ad. Everyone wanted to see the famous missing parakeet. Rosie watched, too, even though the ad made her cry. It was hard seeing Winky on TV when she didn't have him in real life.

When people weren't watching Winky on television, they were calling Rosie to see if she had found him yet.

On Sunday afternoon, the telephone rang for the tenth time. Rosie picked up the receiver.

"No!" she said. "I haven't found my bird."

There was a moment of silence on the line. Then a woman's voice said gently, "Yes, I know. But I think I may have found him."

"What?" cried Rosie. "Where? Is he okay?"

"I think you should hurry," said the woman. "I don't know how long he'll stay."

Shortly afterwards, Aunt Maria was speeding north on the highway toward New York City. Rosie, Michael, and Eliza were in the back seat of the car.

"Do you really think it's Winky?" Rosie asked.

"I don't know," said Aunt Maria. "Mrs. Simmons, the woman who called, said it was dim inside the house and she couldn't see the bird very well.

"I wonder how Winky got to New York," said Michael.

"I don't care how he got there," said Rosie. "All I care about is getting him back."

Soon they were driving through the tunnel and along the streets of New York City. Mrs. Simmons lived in an old townhouse near a small park. She was standing outside, waiting for them.

"Where is he? Where's Winky?" Rosie cried as she jumped out of the car.

"He's upstairs somewhere," said Mrs. Simmons. "I tried to catch him, but he flew away."

Rosie hurried into the house. Michael and Eliza were close behind.

"Don't get your hopes up, Rosie," Aunt Maria called after her. "The bird might not be Winky."

But Rosie's hopes were already as high as the Empire State Building. It was too late to bring them down now.

It was dark and quiet inside the house after the bright, bustling city. Rosie stood for a moment, letting her eyes get used to the dim light.

"You children go on upstairs," Mrs. Simmons said. "I don't want to frighten him again."

Rosie, Michael, and Eliza tiptoed quietly up the stairs.

"Winky, where are you?" Rosie called softly.

Suddenly she heard a sound from the second-floor landing.

"Cheep!"

Rosie raced up to the landing. There, on a

window sill beneath a wide, fan-shaped window, sat a parakeet.

"Winky?" said Rosie, stepping closer. "Winky, is that you?"

But the next moment, Rosie's high hopes came crashing down.

"That parakeet is green," said Eliza. "It's not Winky Blue at all."

Winky Blue Forever

"That parakeet isn't green," said Michael. "It's red."

"It's not red," said Rosie. "Look. It's gold."

Michael stared. "That bird is *all* colors. It's like a rainbow."

Each time the bird moved, it turned a different color. First it was green, then red, and now a brilliant gold.

"It's a magic bird," whispered Eliza. "Maybe we really did fly over the rainbow in that balloon."

"No," said Michael. "It's that big stained-glass window!"

Michael was right. The sunlight streaming through the colored glass made the bird appear to change color as it hopped here and there.

At that moment the rainbow-colored parakeet looked at Rosie, opened its beak, and said, "I love you, Rosie!"

"Winky!" cried Rosie. "I found you!"

Before they started home, Mrs. Simmons handed Rosie a paper bag. Inside was her Winky Blue sweatshirt.

"My husband found your sweatshirt in the back of his truck," Mrs. Simmons explained. "When I saw the bird's picture, I made up my mind to keep a sharp eye out for it. But I never really expected to find your parakeet."

"Especially so far away in New York City," said Michael.

"New York City. Sitting pretty!" chattered Winky, snuggling up against Rosie's cheek.

The next weekend, Bill Burke took another flight, but not in the hot-air balloon.

"I'm going up in a single engine plane," Bill

told Rosie on the phone. "Be sure you and your friends are in the park Saturday at noon."

As it turned out, the whole town was in the park on Saturday at noon.

The cold snap had finally come and the day was clear and cool. Rosie, Michael, and Eliza were on the swings when they heard a roar overhead. Above them a small plane circled in the sky, trailing a ribbon of white smoke.

Raffles barked wildly at the noisy airplane.

"I bet that's Bill up there," said Rosie, craning her neck.

"Look," said Eliza. "He's looping back the other way."

Michael shaded his eyes from the sun.

"It looks like he's writing something with his plane," he said.

Slowly the letters formed. Everyone looked up to read Bill's sky message.

"Ohhh!" gasped Rosie, gazing at the white letters against the blue sky. They were the most beautiful letters she had ever seen.

Rosie thought about how wonderful it was to have Winky back again—not as a hero or a TV star, but as her very own parakeet. Best of all, she thought about all the fun she and Winky would have together, now and forever.

Michael jumped off the swings.

"Come on, let's go down the Slippery Slide," he called as the airplane roared away.

"Coming," Rosie called back.

Before she left, Rosie stopped to take one more look at the sky writing.

"Winky Blue forever," she whispered as the letters faded slowly back to blue. "Winky Blue forever FAMOUS!"